The Short Road

N. Rae

This book is a work of fiction.

An Elocin Press Book
www.elocinpress.com
Copyright 2017 N. Rae
Cover photo by N. Rae
ISBN-13: 978-0-9992135-0-6
ISBN-10: 0999213504

*for*
my family

It began with a recurring nightmare. In the dream, Sophie's playing by herself in the front yard. Skipping rope. Two men drive by slowly in a dark-green four-door car. Dinged and dented. The men slow the car to an impossible crawl. The passenger-side door swings open, a man reaches out, scoops her up, pulls her in. He shoves her to the back seat. The car continues down the street, curves at the cul-de-sac, cruises slowly by her house again. She sees her mother walk out the front door, calling for her. Sophie, on her knees, bangs on the back window of the car, but her mother doesn't look in her direction.

The dream was always soundless. Always slow. It continued for most of third grade. The dark-green car moved at the speed of the tick of the second hand of the clock beside her bed. The colors of the dream were washed away. Her mother, standing on the grass of the front yard, seemed as if she were projected onto a flimsy movie screen. As if they were in different realities. Different dreams.

Sophie would wake from the nightmare into the darkness of her bedroom. The kitten posters on her walls covered by shadows of tree branches moving in the night breeze. The house particularly quiet. All alone in her bed. Afraid to move. She stayed as still as she could, breathing as shallowly as possible with her heart pounding away. Her eardrums aching with a hard, fast pulse.

One night, while still in the dream, she said to her dreaming self: *this is that terrible dream again.* She looked around the world of her sleeping mind. The dream happened as it always happened. Except she was aware of having already been here, of having already done this. She was standing at the edge of the driveway. She saw the green car. When she was in the back seat of the car, she didn't bang on the window this time. She sat on her knees, looking out the back, watching her mother looking for her, soundlessly calling out her name. Dreaming Sophie was thinking, *Please look my way, please.*

Another time during the dream, Sophie willingly sat in the back seat of the strangers' car, arms crossed in front of her chest, refusing to watch her mother calling out for her. Sophie looked closely at the men. Their dirty, messed-up hair. Their unclean, ripped clothing. They were not part of her waking world.

Sophie didn't want to ever get into that car again, so the next time she found herself dreaming at the edge of her driveway, she dropped her skipping rope and ran down the street before the car even appeared. But this world was thick and without air. Her movement was slow and difficult. As the car approached and the door opened, she went up, as if someone above had grabbed the back of her pants and pulled her right out of her dream body which fell to the street. She continued to rise into the sky. The car stopped. Both doors opened. The men stepped out. They looked up at her in the sky, but not at the body collapsed near their feet. They shielded their eyes from the bright sunshine. The car got smaller, the men as tiny as ants. Her street down below getting farther away, her backyard, the brown lake there, her best friend's house, her elementary school. She was floating up into the clouds, into thin air and darkness, all the way into the outer band just beyond the earth. She looked around, frightened. Stranded.

She went back down, moving and behaving as if she were swimming underwater—holding her breath, her cheeks puffed out.

When she returned to her house, it was early morning. She floated down through the roof into her parents' room. She watched them from above. Her father, on the right side of the bed, was lightly snoring, and her mother, on the left side, was awake, reading from the stack of library books on her nightstand. Sophie floated down beside her mother, who shifted slightly as if making room for her. Sophie closed her eyes and fell asleep. When she woke, she was in her own bed. It was Saturday morning. She sat up, looked out her window into the backyard at the lake. The Smith twins were at the shore, writing in the damp dirt with sticks. Sophie got out of bed, went to the garage, grabbed her skipping rope, rolled it up, put it in a plastic bag and then into the large, dank-smelling trash bin.

From that time on, whenever she found herself at the edge of her driveway with the skipping rope in her hands, she would drop the rope and float up into the sky before the car could appear, and she'd travel her town during the night. She would visit her friends who were asleep in bed. One time her friend Camila was awake with the lights off, playing a card game under the covers, a flashlight at her side.

At school the next day on her way to sharpen her pencil, Sophie said, "I saw you last night."

Camila looked up from her desk. "Where?"

"In bed. You were playing solitaire."

Camila looked at Sophie suspiciously. "So?"

Sophie shrugged.

Sophie realized that instead of falling asleep each night, she could leave her body and travel. She would float away each evening on a quiet, observant adventure. She did it so often at bedtime, she found that she could easily do the same thing during the day. While sitting at her desk during class. Or while watching TV. She'd close her eyes and see herself at the edge of the driveway, holding the rope, and she'd drop it and float up into the sky and fly.

Flying during the daytime was much better than flying at night since everyone was awake and doing things. Sometimes her friends were fighting with their siblings. Or eating candy. Playing video games. One time she saw Robert picking his nose, looking at the booger at the end of his finger, then eating it. She liked watching her friends when they were alone. That's when they were the most interesting.

During school the next day, she'd whisper in her friends' ears things she'd seen them doing—while out at recess or walking by them in the classroom. "You eat your boogers." "You stole your sister's math book. You should put it back." She knew she had really seen what she'd seen by the look of shock on their faces. That was exciting. It made her blood rush. The kids nicknamed her Goosebumps. She didn't mind. It wasn't malicious. It was factual.

During sixth grade, Sophie stopped visiting her classmates. She stopped revealing to them the secret things they were doing because they were doing things that embarrassed her. One boy she didn't know very well, an eighth grader, walked up to her in the hallway and said, "Did you see what I did last night? Did you?" He grabbed his crotch.

Sophie still wanted to travel, but she thought leaving her town would be best. Visiting places she had never been. Observing people she didn't know. She decided a good rule was to watch people only when they were with other people. Every day after school when she arrived home, as she was walking up the stairs to her bedroom, she'd tell her mother she was taking a nap. She'd get into her bed, pull the covers up, turn on her side, rise up from her body, and visit Hong Kong, Manhattan, Mexico City. She enjoyed watching people living their lives. Strangers. Never breaking her rule of not watching people when they were alone. Although it was sometimes very difficult not to follow someone into privacy.

Around this time she took to drawing. She'd draw the cities she visited. The faces of the people she had seen. She filled her lined spiral-bound notebooks with faces. Instead of inequalities, her math graph paper was covered with cities seen from above.

\*\*\*

The summer before high school, Sophie's parents divorced. Her father kept the house and moved his girlfriend and her three children in, while Sophie and her mother moved out of suburbia and into a more urban area, into a high-rise community near the Los Angeles County Museum of Art. It was a one-bedroom apartment on the tenth floor. The view from the windows was lovely. Up here, Sophie felt like she could breathe.

She slept on a pullout sofa bed in the living room. Every morning she closed her bed and organized the room as if she had never slept there, and each night she opened her bed as if she were opening her dreaming mind.

She enjoyed being in a new place with new people. She walked to and from school each day. She made no friends. She ate lunch alone in the shade of a tree in the corner near the parking lot and spent her time sketching. By now, she'd realized how special this ability to leave her body was and kept it to herself.

Once every month, her mother would take her to a different art store and let her buy sixty dollars' worth of art supplies. They'd drive to North Hollywood or Santa Monica or as far as San Diego. Her mother would ask questions of the person behind the counter while Sophie sauntered around the store, selecting things and keeping track of what everything cost. She experimented with every medium. By her senior year of high school, Sophie focused on acrylics. She preferred the look of oils, but they took too long to dry and were more expensive.

***

For college, Sophie studied fine art. She spent as much of her time painting as she could. She took public transportation to school. She worked in the college library and as an assistant to a teacher working with hearing-impaired kids. Sophie taught the art class. It was fun working with children. She was a slow sign language speaker and reader, but everyone was patient with her and kind. She could never bring the words alive with her hands as everyone else could. She would practice late at night while in bed with the lights out, trying to conjure emotion with the movement of her hands.

She enjoyed her classes. She tried black-and-white photography. Her favorite part was placing the paper in the solution and watching the image come into being. The image was already there but not able to be seen. She loved that. The photos she took, though—she didn't like those at all.

She took a creative writing class. That was brutal. It took forever to find something to write about, then it took even longer to write a paragraph, and then a group of people spent thirty minutes ripping what you wrote. No thank you.

Painting, on the other hand, was easy. All she had to do was put a little paint on her brush, and what happened next just happened. It was like she was watching herself.

She enjoyed staying up late into the night working on her assignments. Sometimes she was invited to do group shows but not as often as her classmates. She tried to create some group shows of her own, but her fellow students were always already busy. She watched everyone else advance; they got representation or solo shows or job offers, while nothing seemed to be happening for her.

She went to her favorite teacher's office and asked for some advice. The teacher sat back in her chair, folded her hands over her belly, and said, "Here's the truth. You paint portraits and cities. It's just not exciting." Sophie listened as her teacher went on for the next ten minutes. It was excruciating. As Sophie was leaving, the teacher stretched, put her hands behind her head, and said, "And your name. It's cute but not professional. It's time to change it. You're not a little kid anymore."

***

After college, Sophie got a job at an Italian restaurant waiting tables. She had seen an ad on craigslist. When she walked in the door, there were waiters and waitresses standing around in white tuxedo tops, black bow ties, and black pants. There was an older man, very thin and dapper, in a suit and tie. Next to him was a short woman in a very orange dress. The dapper older man had a strong Italian accent. He said, "What do you want?"

"I saw the craigslist ad for a waiter."

He said, "If you take off your clothes, the job is yours."

"If I what?"

The woman in the orange dress said, "Your coat! Your coat! Take off your coat!"

She took off her coat.

***

Sophie worked the lunch shift Tuesday through Saturday and made enough money to spend the rest of her time painting. All the other waiters and waitresses were trying to break into the movies in one way or another. Since Sophie was a painter and not seen as competition, she was well liked and never treated dubiously, which was how they treated one another.

***

It was dark out. Sophie stood at the kitchen window, looking down at the courtyard of their apartment complex. The fog was moving in. Her mother asked her if she'd set the table yet.

Sophie opened the drawer next to the fridge and took out two placemats and two fabric napkins. Her mother opened the take-out containers and scooped food onto their plates with the cheap wooden chopsticks. It was just after midnight. They walked out to the living room together.

Sophie ate as she flipped through a fashion magazine, while her mother, grinning, just moved her food around her plate.

"Sophie! Aren't you going to ask me why I'm so happy?"

She looked up from her magazine. "What?"

"I met a man."

"You did?"

Her mother had been trying to fall madly in love for years. But it never worked out. If her mother had been dumped, she would come home from the date, intoxicated, and undress as she walked to her bedroom, leaving her clothes on the floor, saying, "It's harder for women."

"Where did you meet this man?"

"On the Internet."

"OK."

"He lives in Berlin."

"Germany?"

"Yes. That Berlin." Her mother pointed the chopsticks at her. "Don't make that face. Anyway, I'm going to move there."

"OK."

"You stay here."

"I'll stay here."

"Good." Her mother smiled. "If it doesn't work out, I'll come back. I think it'll work."

"But meeting someone in person is different. You might not like him at all."

"We've met."

"When?"

"I don't have to tell you everything."

"You should probably tell me something."

But her mother wouldn't tell her anything more than that. The only other thing her mother said was, "You're ready to be on your own now. You'll be fine."

Sophie cleaned up her food, tossed what was left of her takeout into the kitchen trash, looked at her magazine, then threw that out as well.

The next week, her mother moved out. She was so eager she couldn't stand still. She'd clap her hands at odd moments. Sophie was happy for her, although she felt sad for herself. She felt abandoned. And lonely. She'd never felt loneliness before.

She looked up her mother's address in Berlin on the Internet, zooming in and out of the satellite map. She looked at the path she would take if she were to fly there in her other body. She spent a little time every day imagining this. She'd never tried to go to an exact location before. She didn't really know how to do it.

Two weeks after her mother left the country, Sophie got into bed in the daylight and rose out of her body and traveled to her mother. It was nighttime in Berlin. Which was not what she had practiced. She was thrown off. Nothing looked familiar. She spent time looking and searching and learning. She flew high above the dark city, as high as a plane. The electric lights created pathways, and the city looked like a dendrite—alive and full of information.

Unable to sleep that same night, Sophie left her body again and returned to Berlin. It was early in the morning now. She spent hours there walking around, orienting herself to the layout of the city. Although people passed her on the street, she couldn't ask them for directions. Just before she was about to give up, she found two streets intersecting that she recognized. She found her mother's building. She rose up into the air, circled the building, peeking into windows, and then there was her mother on the fourth floor, in her new apartment, happily speaking with a man. They were holding hands across a small round table. Sophie watched them for a short time, then flew back across the ocean, across her country, back into her city, her body, and woke.

She stayed in bed and thought about how time moved when she was outside her physical self. It was the same time as when she was awake, but she could travel so quickly in it that it seemed like a different time altogether.

Eventually, unable to sleep, Sophie got out of bed.

She opened up her laptop, went to YouTube, and watched videos about Berlin. Clicking on one suggested video after another, each one connected to but different from the last, and soon she was watching a horror movie called *The Old Dark House*. When it was over, she immediately watched it again. She liked the opening sequence. The three people in the car, driving through the rainstorm, bickering. How dark the set was—such low visibility. You could tell it was a set, but an extravagant one, filled with mud, fake rain and sliding earth.

That day, she had a strong desire to paint. Images from the film were pressing on her mind: the dark open rooms, the fancy interlopers, the quirky isolated family, the witty dialogue—all of it uncontrollably moved through her thoughts. She had hardly begun one painting when she wanted to start another. And then another. She decided that she could capture more if she sketched her ideas out. She filled a book.

After completing or losing interest in one painting, she'd sort through her sketchbook and pick something else. She signed her name on the bottom right of each canvas as *Sophia*. That seemed like the name of a professional.

The paintings hung on the wall just above the sofa bed where she used to sleep. She had twenty so far, various sizes, various stages of completion. Dark blues. Dark greens. Black, gray, brown. She'd continued to watch *The Old Dark House* every day, speaking all the parts absentmindedly as she painted.

All the while she became more aware of an emptiness inside her. With each painting, it became more pronounced. She didn't know what to do with it. Sometimes she thought she was trying to paint the emptiness out of being.

Her daily life took on a pattern. She'd get home from waiting tables around 4:00 p.m., close all the drapes in her bedroom, take a shower, put on her pajamas, put her noise-canceling earbuds in, place an eye mask over her eyes, and get into bed. The soundlessness and darkness enveloped her. She'd breathe deeply, let her belly fill up, then hold her breath for ten seconds. Then she'd exhale, sucking her belly in until all the air was out of her body, hold her breath, then breathe in. Soon her body would feel as if she were floating out on a waterless ocean. Her body becoming one with the motion. Within a few minutes she would be released from herself, rise up, then turn, and watch herself in bed, that body there not exactly sleeping as her different body, here, floated above. She'd move through the ceiling or the walls or go down through the floor and off into the world. Once she awakened from her adventure, she'd search out an old black-and-white horror film to watch on YouTube, make herself something to eat, then paint or study.

At around midnight, she'd clean her brushes, put things away, brush her teeth, and go to bed. Sometimes she would fly in the night; other times she would not. She welcomed the night flying, but since she had already done it during the day, she wasn't reliant on it.

***

On this particular night, her neck aching, she stopped working on the portrait of Gloria Stuart as Margaret Waverton in the long silky white dress from *The Old Dark House*. Sophia had been really trying to get the sheen of the fabric, but rendering the reality of cloth had never been a strong area for her. She hung the painting on her cluttered wall, cleaned her brushes, brushed her teeth, got into bed, and quickly fell into a deep sleep.

She awoke in space between the moon and the earth. It was similar to being nowhere. It was very still. There was no temperature. Everything felt thin. It felt like being trapped under a bell jar.

Leaving her body had never happened in this way before. She had never suddenly appeared somewhere.

She wondered how she got here. Where she had been, if anywhere. She turned to see a person behind her, floating as she was floating, the white-gray moon outlining the person's form. The figure seemed male. She called out to him, but there was no sound. She moved forward, away from him, and he soon followed as if they were attached by a string. She went left, and he soon went left. She went up, and he soon went up. She turned and went toward him. He didn't move.

His eyes were open but unaware. He was handsome. He had on a dark-blue T-shirt and faded jeans. He was pretty. Her age. Muscular but not large. She reached out and touched his hand. His body was warm. She looked around for someone else. There was no one. She searched the universe, suspecting there might be an eye looking through a keyhole camouflaged as a galaxy.

She observed the stillness of hanging in the void of space. She could feel herself breathing in the darkness of her bed as an extension of her sleeping body. And that this body made those same motions, her lungs seeming to expand and deflate, but was not actually breathing. The milk-white shine of the glowing moon illuminated part of his face. She turned to gaze at the pretty green and blue of the full round earth. She looked around again for someone else—for that eye spying through a peephole—then she kissed him ever so gently on his soft, warm lips. He didn't respond. She hugged him. His body warm, although he wasn't breathing. She pressed two fingers into his neck just below his jaw. Her fingertips pressed against stubble. There was a pulse, slow and dragging. She swam away from him, and he followed. As she entered the earth's atmosphere, she felt for the rope that must be connecting them but didn't find it. She spun in the thin air, and after a slight delay, he swung out and was pulled toward her. She caught his arm and brought him snug up to her side, taking him down with her to the top of Mount Denali in the early morning. It was very calm and still. Hushed.

She said to him, "It's beautiful, isn't it?"

He didn't speak. His eyes open, but not seeing. His body warm but not moving. She wrapped her arms around herself to protect against the cold that could not harm her. Other mountaintops were peeking through the wispy clouds. The snow on the mountains reminded her of shaving cream. She pointed and turned to tell him to look over there, but he was no longer beside her. The next moment she was standing on her bed, eyes open, the bright, creamy sunshine coming in her windows. She stayed completely still, moving only her eyes to take in the room.

*** 

A few days later, while walking home from work, she thought she saw the man from space looking at her from a window of a bus passing by.

*** 

Each afternoon after returning from work, she would take her nap, float to space, and look for him. He was never there. She would stop painting early each evening and go to bed in hopes of finding him, traveling the outer reaches, zooming around the moon in search of him.

*** 

Her coworker Julia wanted to go to an audition, so Sophia stayed on at the restaurant during the lull between three and five. She was transferring the glasses from the kitchen to the bar when she noticed someone sitting at a table in the far corner near the windows. His back to her. She grabbed her pad from her apron pocket, and as she walked toward him, she realized the person sitting there was the man from space. A light sweat broke out between her breasts and just above her lip. She slowed her steps as she wiped the back of her hand across her mouth. She kept her gaze on the floor, on the large black-and-white squares of tile. She stopped when she got to the table. She put her pencil to her pad and said, "What can I get you?"

His shoes were brown penny loafers. No socks. He had nice ankles.

"I'd like a glass of water."

His voice was deep. A little scratchy. Hollow sounding as if it were coming from a great distance.

She returned with a glass of water, set it on the table, and went back to the bar.

She watched him as she set the glasses on the shelf. He did not drink.

When Luis arrived to take over, as he was tying his apron around his waist, he asked what she was thinking about.

"Nothing."

"You had such a faraway look."

She shrugged.

"I get that way too when the place is empty."

Luis walked over to the table in the far corner. He picked up the glass of water and smoothed the tablecloth. He didn't acknowledge or seem to be aware that a man was sitting there. Sophia touched her face. Her hands were cold, and her skin was hot. She felt faint.

\*\*\*

After that, she saw the man from space constantly. At the grocery store. The corner convenience store. Riding on buses. Sitting on benches. Each afternoon during her nap she went out looking for him in the ether, but could never find him out there.

Early one Sunday morning, when she opened the

window near her bed, she saw him far down below on the street. Standing on the sidewalk, looking up at her.

She called down to him, "Do you want to come inside?"

He said he did.

She rode the elevator down and walked him through the courtyard and into the building, up the elevator. She opened the front door. He waited.

"Go in," she said.

He stepped over the threshold, turned, and watched her walk in.

"That was easy," he said.

"It's just a doorway," she said.

He seemed real, but she knew he wasn't; at the same time, she was certain he was. He didn't touch things with his hands. He could appear to sit or stand. He was wearing clothes. His body now wasn't like the body when they were floating. But his body wasn't like hers. She couldn't touch him. He gave off no heat. He looked solid enough, but if she tilted her head just so and he turned his body just so, the edge of him disappeared.

He sat on her sofa with a cup of hot green tea before him that he wouldn't handle or drink, but that he had requested. She sat across from him in an armchair with her legs tucked up to her chest, holding her mug of tea in both hands. He asked her a series of questions, and she answered them. Whenever she asked a question, he would respond with a question.

His tea had cooled long ago. He said, "I guess I should go now."

She stood up. "Could we meet tonight? Like we met the first time."

"When was that?"

"When I saw you up there?"

"Where?"

"We stood on top of Denali."

He shook his head.

"The mountain?"

He shrugged.

"Tonight, when it's dark, I'll be on the roof of this building waiting for you. You should meet me there."

He nodded. She leaned over to get his cup from the coffee table, and when she stood up, he was gone.

She passed the evening flipping through books and magazines, watching clips of horror movies on YouTube, while keeping her eye on the time. She got into bed: eye mask, earbuds, deep breathing. It took longer than usual, but she did lift out of herself, rolling over at the ceiling and looking down on her sleeping body. She pulled herself up and through the ceiling, passing the bedroom of the people who lived above her. The lights were on, the king bed was not made, and there were no people in the room. She could hear music coming from down the hallway. She reached that ceiling, grabbed on, and pulled herself through and into the next room, which was dark, then through that ceiling and onto the roof of the building. He was already waiting for her there.

They looked out at the city sprawl. If they went left on Wilshire Boulevard, it would take them downtown; a right would take them to the ocean. There wasn't much traffic. There was a helicopter far over to the east, running its searchlight on the ground. The wind was quite strong. It moved through them as if they were open windows.

"You're more like me now," he said.

They stood there awkwardly.

"What should we do?" he asked.

"What do you want to do?"

"What is there to do?"

If he were real, they could do all sorts of things. She could take him to a movie, and they could eat popcorn and candy and drink sodas. They could ride roller coasters. Sit at a café and drink coffee. She could take him to see a concert. Which they could still do. But it occurred to her that maybe the way they were communicating wasn't based on sound.

"Can you hear me?"

He smirked. "Yes."

"Do you hear the traffic on the ten over there? Or that car alarm beeping down there?"

They looked over the edge of the building down to the street below just as the beeping stopped.

"I can hear those two people talking."

Two teenagers were leaning against a car, chatting, laughing, sharing a cigarette.

"Can you smell the cigarette?"

"Yes. I like it."

She took his hand in hers. He let out a sound of surprise. She could feel his skin the way you can feel the temperature of a hot object before you actually touch it.

She said, "Let's go this way." She lifted off and took him in the direction of the ocean. "That's the tar pits. But let's go this way." She pulled him to the right. "This is the Farmers Market. And that's CBS." She dragged him along. "I graduated from high school there. If you could eat food, we'd have cheesecake there. It's so good. Especially if you let it sit out on your windowsill overnight wrapped in foil and then the sunshine heats it up in the morning and the sugar crystalizes." She took him all around, ending at the Greek Theatre, thinking they could watch a concert, but it was over, and the instruments were being packed up. Still, it was fun to sit up in the rafters and watch.

"Should we go to the ocean?"

"I would love to."

They held hands and flew off into the night, up high into the clouds and then down to the darkness of the water, the sound of waves coming up onto shore and then the water pulling back into itself. The ray of white moonlight across the blue-black water. The wet beach, with wet rocks. People were camping in vehicles, deeply sleeping inside them. They sat there on the rocks at the water, watching and listening to the waves. Sophia was having a slight sensation of air rustling along her vague body. It was tranquil and sweet.

"Will you come see me tomorrow? I'm home all day."

"Yes." He kissed her cheek. She could feel the warmth of him but nothing else. The next moment, she awoke in her bed in the early morning, happy and rested.

They spent each day together. When she napped, they spent that time together too. She said she preferred that time, and he said he liked it all. She asked him about himself, and he said he didn't know. That there was nothing before or after this.

It was wonderful to have him with her. He added to her day, never distracting from it. He didn't have any bodily needs that she was aware of. He didn't have any needs at all. He was like an extension of her mind. It was similar to talking to herself in her head but more like talking to someone else inside herself, as if the world outside her was mirrored by another world inside.

When Sophia was out in public, she put her earbuds in and pretended that she was talking on the phone. She called him Andy. She was always on the phone with Andy. Everyone at the restaurant was interested in him. He should come by. Sorry, she said, that wasn't possible. She met him online. He lived in Canada. Luis said, "Really? Canada? Really?"

***

At around this time, she made friends with a woman named Lydia, a café owner, who had run inside the restaurant to get out of a sudden downpour. Lydia sat at the bar, ordered a glass of red wine, and patted her face dry with cocktail napkins. Lydia said, "Nice weather for ducks."

"That's a line from a movie I'm obsessed with," Sophia said, setting the glass of wine before Lydia.

"What movie's that?"

"It's an old horror film from the early thirties."

"It's not *The Old Dark House*, is it?"

"Yes!"

"With Boris Karloff."

"Is that Boris Karloff?"

"It says so in the beginning of the film."

"OK."

"And Charles Laughton's in it."

"Which one's he?"

Lydia tilted her head. "Are you kidding?"

"All I know is that I really like the way the crazy old sister eats her food."

"That would be Eva Moore. So, you don't know who Raymond Massey is, either?"

"Are we going to play this game all day?"

They chatted about that movie and famous actors, the women's suffrage movement, and Laurence Olivier. Sophia wrote down some films that Lydia recommended.

After Lydia left, Luis said, "Oh my God. You just made a real friend."

"Shut up."

"And she lives right here in LA."

Sophia rolled her eyes.

"She's a little old for you," Luis said, "but we'll take what we can get. Right?"

\*\*\*

Lydia showed up a few days later wearing what she always wore: black jeans, gray T-shirt, black Converse shoes. She sat at the bar and drank a glass of wine and talked about old Hollywood movies.

"OK," Lydia said, "You want to watch something really weird?"

"Probably not."

"It's OK. It's not modern-day, wash-your-eyes-out-with-bleach weird. They're strange and beautiful and creepy old films on YouTube that are sort of home-movieish. Freaky. Like satanic-ritual kind of stuff? Orgies."

Sophia wrote down the three movies. "I don't know if I will."

"They're really beautiful and eerie. They're so weird. So, so weird."

\*\*\*

Lydia dropped by a few days a week. She'd eat lunch at the bar and always leave too large a tip. Sometimes Andy would be sitting on a barstool next to Lydia, but Sophia couldn't interact with him while she was interacting with Lydia, so he would be silent and watchful.

On her way home from work, Sophia would go by Lydia's café, which was in the opposite direction of Sophia's home, just down Olympic, but not too out of the way. She'd stand at the espresso bar and drink whatever Lydia gave her.

***

"I need a really tall glass of wine," Lydia said. "Fill it all the way."

"What kind?"

"Any kind."

Sophia had just opened a bottle of Chianti. Sophia placed a cocktail napkin in front of Lydia, then the glass, then filled it up. Lydia smiled, leaned in, and sipped the wine until she could lift the glass without spilling. "Perfect." Lydia quietly drank her wine. Sophia didn't ask any questions. When the glass was empty, Lydia ordered lunch.

"Tell me a story."

"I don't have any. You want another glass of wine?"

"No. Give me some fizzy water. Hey, I want to see some of your paintings."

Sophia opened a bottle of Perrier, setting it on another cocktail napkin. She took the wine glass away. She opened her phone and showed Lydia photos of the paintings she'd made that were inspired by *The Old Dark House*.

"These are great. You know, you can have a show at my café, if you want. It's a good space."

"No! That's OK."

"Let's do it."

"Are you sure?"

Of course she was sure. When Lydia left, Luis said, "Wow, that was easy."

Sophia, who had been trying to do just that thing for years now, said, "Not really, no."

***

Lydia arrived at Sophia's apartment the next day and selected twelve paintings.

"What do you want to call your show?"

"That's always hard for me. What do you think?"

"These are all the same inspiration?"

"Yes."

"So maybe something based off the title of the film? *Scenes from* The Old Dark House."

"OK."

"No, that's terrible. God." Lydia shook her head. "So, the film is dark. Sinister. Hidden."

"But it's also cute."

"There's a storm."

"There's a madman locked in the attic," Sophia said.

"That's right. The little crazy guy who lights the curtains on fire. You know, the person in the attic is usually a crazy old hag. So that's interesting. Do you have a painting of him?"

"No, but I could. The flames would be nice. It could be the one bit of bright color. Put that painting in the center to the right, down here. The mouth of hell."

"Yeah, do that."

Sophia crossed her arms. "What's hidden in the shadows? What's locked in the attic?"

Lydia pointed at the large painting of Rebecca Femm and Margaret Waverton, both naked and hunched over with a pretty script of writing at the bottom: *This is nice, but it will rot.* Lydia said, "That's the scene where the old lady is telling the young lady about the dead sister and saying how the house was full of laughter and sin."

They talked about the thrill of horror movies. How these old movies were a fun type of scary with an edge of the sinister.

"So, we want the fun and the dark?"

"What about *Fun in the Dark*?"

"There you go."

"There you go."

Sophia gave Lydia an artist statement from a previous group show from when she was in college. Lydia read it over, then carefully and precisely folded it in half, and handed it back. "Let me write your artist statement."

\*\*\*

Sophia worked on the painting with Saul, the madman who lived in the attic. He had the torch in his hand. He was lighting the curtains on fire. She painted it from one of the camera angles in the film, looking through the fireplace with flames on the left and the right. She placed Saul to the left of the canvas, deep into the room, far away, cackling, fancy script of *hee hee hee ha ha*.

Andy kept her company as she worked. He was never tired. Never hungry. He would come and go without warning.

"Where do you go when you're gone?"

He didn't know.

"Then why do you go?"

"I just feel like leaving, and then I'm not here."

"You must be somewhere."

"I guess."

*** 

Andy was with her while she hung her paintings at Lydia's café. Sophia ignoring him in public as usual. She thought that she might be a little crazy, and it bothered her that it was only suddenly occurring to her that he might not be real—that this might all be happening in her crazed, lonely mind rather than in a convergence of realities.

The more she ignored him in public, the more she ignored him in private, and the less often he came to visit. She stopped napping in the afternoon because she didn't want to see him in that world and have to ignore him there as well. That world became his domain, although she believed that he wasn't an authentic part of that world. She just happened to find him there. She didn't know where he belonged, and she didn't want to think about it anymore.

***

A somewhat-famous Hollywood actor frequented Lydia's café each day to get his morning cappuccino. He'd stand at the bar with the other patrons, drink his cappuccino, and eat a banana while chatting with everyone. They liked to hear him talk about other more famous people. He never named names, and he never told a nasty story. He did good imitations, and it was easy to guess who everyone was. He was fun. In the middle of a charming anecdote, he stopped, looked around, and said, "What the hell are these things?"

He walked around the café, looking over Sophia's paintings. He wasn't particularly a fan of horror films or old Hollywood movies, but he liked the paintings. He said his sister had a gallery at Bergamot Station. He took some photos and texted them to his sister.

The sister liked the paintings and offered to represent Sophia. She said she could easily include her art in an upcoming show at her gallery two months from now and that she'd been looking for exciting new blood. She put four of Sophia's paintings on their website. It was amusing how easy it seemed afterward. Sophia had been trying for years to find someone to represent her. When it finally happened, it was like turning on a light, and she forgot about the darkness and all that fumbling around.

***

A few weeks after this, Sophia was setting up the kitchen for the people on the next shift—making sure there were salads in the fridge, that all the dressings were full, those sorts of things—when Luis and two other coworkers came in early to tell her about a film idea they had. A horror flick inspired by Sophia's paintings that were hanging in Lydia's café. They had already rented a warehouse out in the Valley. They asked Sophia to design the set and paint the portraits that would hang on the walls of the spooky old mansion. They had an excellent cast of actors, which included them, and a fantastic script, which they wrote. They'd put the film up on YouTube when they were done.

Sophia was so busy waiting tables and designing sets, painting *trompe l'oeil* backdrops as well as detailed, storybook-establishing shots, and old-style portraits of the characters and their ancestors, that she forgot about Andy.

Filming the movie was very exciting. Sophia stood behind the director to watch. All sorts of different cameras were involved. Digital, 16 mm, smartphones. Everyone on set had a camera directed somewhere at some point except for her. None of them were being paid for their time, but they were all ready to give whatever they could. Most everything was borrowed or donated. And things that needed to be paid for were purchased on credit. There was a little bowl of maxed-out, canceled, and cut-in-half credit cards on the table by the doughnuts and coffee.

The director would often clap his hands, vigorously rub them together, and say, "I hope this works out."

***

The horror film got a little bit of recognition. They were proud of it. It was amusing and spooky and beautiful. Lots of witty banter among the characters. Well-acted. Truly delightful. It was also quirky, and it lingered a little in your mind afterward. You did wonder about the world in which you lived.

The success of the short film led to Sophia selling a few paintings, which allowed her to pay off an enormous amount of student debt as well as save a little money. She felt very comfortable financially for the first time in her life, but her desire to paint was gone. There was nothing in her mind. It was a bright whiteness when she closed her eyes. It was blinding. There was no obsession pressing on her.

She called her mother, hoping to have a decent conversation, but her mother didn't like to talk on the phone, and being far away didn't change that. Sophia asked when her mother would be coming back to town, but her mother said she didn't know. Sophia asked when she might get to meet her mother's boyfriend, and her mother said, "Sweetie, I have no idea. Please stop asking."

***

Sophia waited tables as usual, but after she got home from her shift, she'd sit in her apartment and waste time. She'd search the Internet, trying to find something to interest her, but not one thing created a passion inside her.

She tried a new strategy. She got out the ladder and hung a number of empty canvases on her wall and stared at the blank spaces. She pulled the sofa away from the wall and put it against the windows. She measured the wall. She took down all the preframed canvases and pulled the nails out of the wall with pliers. She purchased enough loose canvas to fully cover the wall, then cut it into all shapes and sizes and stitched it together with thick black embroidery floss. She thought of it as her monster. She nailed the large stitched canvas to her wall, covering the entire space. She'd sit on the floor and just stare at her monster and scratch her head. What to do with it. What to do.

She dragged her mattress out to the living room so that when she woke, her monster was the first thing she saw.

She went on long walks along the streets. She'd walk down Fairfax to Hollywood Boulevard to La Brea and home.

After one such walk, she stopped in at Erewhon to get juice and a little something from the deli. As she was walking around, she spotted Andy at the flowers. She walked up beside him, leaned over some beautiful daffodils, and said without looking at him, "I've missed you."

He took a step away.

She looked up at him and smiled. He walked around to the other side of the flowers, trying not to make eye contact. She followed him. "Are you mad at me?" He turned and walked deeper into the store. She followed. "I understand if you're angry. I do." He moved a little faster. She followed.

In the wine aisle, he turned to her and said, "Do I know you?"

His voice wasn't like Andy's. She stepped back. She walked around him, trying to catch the edge of him disappearing, but his edges were very sharp and clean. She stepped up to him and grabbed his arm. He pulled his arm away, stepping back. She looked at her hands.

"I'm so sorry," she said. "Really. I'm so sorry. You look identical—I swear it—identical to someone else." She touched her forehead and laughed. "I'm so embarrassed." She wanted to touch him again. It was thrilling to feel him, to have him in her hands. She wanted to grab him again.

He smiled. "This is the oddest pickup at a grocery store I've ever had."

"This happens to you often?"

"You say that like it's surprising."

"No…I just…you're cute. I'm not saying you're not cute."

"As long as we're not saying that." He walked away.

Sophia stepped into the next aisle and watched him through the items on the shelves. He picked out some cheese, an apple, grapes, and a baguette. She saw him scan the shop for her every minute or so, but she stayed hidden. He looked so much like Andy. So much. When he left the store, she walked over to the cold section and stood there. Her face felt as if it had a sunburn. She held on to the cold things there and then pressed her cold hands to her cheeks and the back of her neck. She put a chocolate bar in her basket while waiting in line. She paid for her things and left the store.

Sitting at the table just outside the store was the guy who looked so much like Andy. He said, "You want to sit? Are you hungry?"

She sat down. She shared her deli salad with him. He'd never had it before and liked it. They didn't say much to each other, but she didn't feel uncomfortable in the silence. It was very hot, but there was a cool breeze, and they were in the shade of the building.

When the food was gone, they cleaned up and walked out into the sun together.

"What's your name?"

She held out her hand. "I'm Sophia."

"I'm Raymond."

They shook hands.

"Where are you headed now?"

"Home."

"Maybe we will see each other again?"

"Maybe."

They stood there for a moment, then parted. She looked over her shoulder. He was already looking at her. He smiled.

"Where do you live, Sophia?"

"I live over there." She pointed to the tall buildings in the distance. "Where do you live?"

He pointed in the opposite direction. "But I'm actually on my way to a job over there." He pointed toward the ocean.

"What sort of job?"

"I build decks and patios. What do you do?"

"I paint and wait tables."

"Houses?"

"Canvases."

He looked down at her feet. "What size shoe do you wear?"

She looked down at her feet. At her sandals. "Eight."

"What's that in a guy size?"

"A six."

"You any good with a hammer?"

"I know how to pound a nail."

"That sounds suggestive."

"If we're talking about building decks, then I guess it is." She put the words *building decks* in air quotes.

"I like you," he said.

"That's because I'm very likable."

"My truck is parked over there. Want to help me build a deck?"

"Why not."

He rummaged behind the driver's seat and pulled out an old pair of work boots.

"They'll be a little big, but they'll be fine."

***

When she was safe at home alone in her bed, she realized that she had driven out into the hills of Malibu with a complete stranger. A complete stranger with bludgeoning tools. She realized she'd done something unwise. This man was not Andy, although he looked amazingly like him. She couldn't say anything other than that about Andy since he didn't really have wants or desires. He didn't have a history. He had no stories. There was nothing really to know about Andy except that he was kind and gentle and sweet. She found herself saying to Raymond things like, "You are so familiar."

"Maybe we've met before."

"Maybe."

"In another life." And he'd laugh.

Sometimes she'd say, "When I brought you down from the heavens to me…"

And he would wrinkle his nose and shake his head. "You mean when you molested me in the grocery store?"

"When I groped you."

"Accosted."

"Waylaid."

"What was that about anyway?"

She shrugged.

"It's good to be so remarkably handsome as I am."

"If only we could all be so lucky."

***

She was inspired to paint him. Sitting naked on the sofa. Standing at the window in a T-shirt and jeans. Holding a bowl of fruit, offering it to the viewer. She took photographs of him throughout the day. She liked to paint him in his dirty work clothes, sweaty and exhausted, sitting on a wall or on the back of his truck, or the deck he was working on with the blue Pacific Ocean in the background. The slash of faint moon in the daylight sky, far off in the distance.

The large canvas she had stitched together was still on her living room wall. Still blank.

"Are you going to ever take this down?"

"Does it bother you?"

"Sort of."

"I'll think about it."

"At least paint something on it. Anything!"

"You're so strange. Just think of it as a wall."

"That's not a wall. It's the monster of all monsters."

***

Raymond enjoyed watching the short film she'd worked on, and he mentioned it to everyone—"Have you seen that horror film Sophia did the art for?" He seemed to go out of his way to chat with people they didn't know and mention the film. "It's on YouTube. You should check it out." It was sweet. But it made her anxious.

As a birthday gift, he bought her a large, heavy, beautiful book about Hollywood backdrops. It gave her crazy feverish ideas, and she kept a notepad and pen with the book at all times. She'd find herself sitting on the floor, looking through the book late at night with her phone's flashlight. She'd write ideas for movies that would never exist and sketch backdrops for them.

***

One evening while at home, eating dinner together, lost in their own thoughts, everything so quiet that the sound of Sophia turning the pages of her magazine made it seem like that was the only sound in the world, Raymond said, "I think we love each other."

She said, "I think we do," and continued eating as if he had said something very simple and obvious.

"I think that's a big deal."

"It is."

"Then why are you acting like I just said it's a nice sunny day?"

"That there is a sun and that it is shining isn't anything to yawn about."

"Yawn." He covered his mouth as if he were yawning.

She ate another bite of food.

He said, "I think we should get married."

34

"That's fine with me."

"You could get all excited or cry or something."

"I'm crying on the inside."

"What if…" he cleared his throat, "I have a ring in my pocket? With rubies in it? And it's very pretty and expensive? Will you cry then?"

"Is it for me?"

"Why would it be for you?"

She frowned. "I'm not smart enough for these philosophical arguments of yours."

He stood up, set his bowl of pasta on the table, and pulled a ring out of his front pocket. He put it on his pinkie finger, sat down, picked up his bowl, looked out the window, and put a forkful of food in his mouth.

She leaned across the table and held out her hand for the pretty ring.

He looked at his pinkie. "It's mighty nice, ain't it?"

"It's remarkable. May I see it?"

He held up his hand and said, "See?"

"Will you please take the ring off your finger and place it in my hand?"

He sighed. "You're what they call a micromanaging harlot."

"You are so rude."

He took the ring off his finger and put it on her left ring finger.

"It fits perfectly," she said.

"Then you must have it," he said. "I insist."

"I couldn't! It's much too expensive."

"Oh, it's a cheap knockoff. Don't worry."

"Is it?"

"No. It's the real thing. I found a fancy-pants

jeweler on Instagram. Handmade. In Seattle."

She turned her hand to him so that he could see the ring. She wiggled her fingers so that the rubies might catch the light and sparkle. "How lucky am I?"

"You are the most lucky."

"It's a good thing I brought you down to me from the heavens."

"It is."

She leaned forward and they kissed. A soft, gentle kiss with just the slightest bit of tongue.

"I love you very much."

"That's good," she said.

\*\*\*

Raymond moved out of his apartment in North Hollywood and in with Sophia. He liked being on the tenth floor of a building. It pleased him to sit on the barstool in her little kitchen, right at the open window, listening to a podcast playing on the little speaker, feeling the cool breeze rushing in while he ate his bowl of cereal in the morning. He could hear the people talking down below, as if they were right next to him. The wind would lift their voices. Sometimes people would be having a fight, teenagers with their parents or couples in love or friends, and he'd turn up the volume of the podcast to give them their privacy.

\*\*\*

Sophia had had a bad week. She tripped while walking home from work and skinned her knee. She spilled salad dressing in some lady's hair. God. She stepped on a grape while delivering a Coke to a table and did a sort of split, injuring her inner thigh. She was also unable to open a bottle of wine, and the woman said, "Put the bottle between your knees. That's what I do."

Sophia put the bottle between her knees, the cork broke, and Luis filmed the whole thing, zooming in on her face. He showed it to everyone in the kitchen. Sophia could hear them laughing about it for the next week.

***

Sophia and Raymond's wedding, which took place in her apartment, was on a nice summer morning among their parents, Raymond's younger sister, and their friend Lydia, who was the officiant. Sophia's mother had come in from Berlin two weeks before and was staying in Torrance with a friend she'd known since elementary school. Sophia's father was not there, but his wife sent them a check for a hundred dollars and wished them the best of luck. Raymond's mom was there with her girlfriend, and Raymond's father was there with his fourth wife, who had a nice easy smile and many funny things to say.

Sophia and Raymond married in front of the monster backdrop, which she'd finally painted.

When Raymond saw it finished he said, "It's like we're astronauts. Or aliens."

There was the moon, big and heavy, glowing bone-white. And then the earth, large and pretty, teeming with life. There were lights set between the wall and the backdrop to make it seem like the earth and the moon were aglow. At night it was a spectacular vision.

"It's for our wedding."

"But that's too big."

"No, it's not."

"It's portentous. Is that the right word? Like something's going to happen. Ominous? It will put a very science fiction sort of spin on our marriage. Don't you think?"

"You don't like it."

He put his hands on his hips. "I like it. It's beautiful. But it's weird. To get married in front of."

"I made it for us." Sophia said it in such a way that meant *if the backdrop came down, then there would be no marriage.*

"I can't wait," said Raymond. "This will be awesome. I love it. Maybe we should get those glass things to put over our heads. So we can breathe."

"We don't need those. We've never needed those."

They stared at each other for some time. Raymond sighed. Sophia crossed her arms over her chest and gritted her teeth.

Sophia wore a long pale-pink dress that they purchased at a consignment shop for one hundred dollars two days before the ceremony. They had already gone into terrible debt to buy Raymond's suit, which they purchased at a fancy shop on Rodeo Drive a month ago. It was a light-gray summer suit that looked very pretty next to her pale-pink wedding gown.

As the guests waited for the couple, who were hiding out in the bedroom, Raymond's sister, Valerie, passed out glasses of fresh-squeezed orange juice.

Sophia's mother stood before the backdrop and said, "This is the most magnificent setting for a wedding I've ever seen."

Raymond's mother said, "Your daughter is very talented."

"Yes. Obviously," said Sophia's mother.

During their vows, Sophia said how glad she was that she found her love out there in the void. Raymond said that the day she violated him at their favorite health food store was the most auspicious day of his life. That he wished he could be so violated every day. She leaned in and whispered, "I'll violate you later tonight if you want."

He leaned in and whispered, "Yes. Thank you."

There was no best man or maid of honor. The photos that Lydia took with just her phone were otherworldly. Everyone toasted afterward with fresh orange juice in champagne flutes and ate homemade chocolate cupcakes with white chocolate frosting that Sophia and Raymond had stayed up the night before making because they couldn't sleep. They had felt like overexcited children.

Raymond's sister said, "You mean to say that there wouldn't have been any celebratory treat if you'd been able to sleep?"

They didn't have enough money to go on a honeymoon. Raymond would say, "Who needs a honeymoon? We were married in space!" And the money they were gifted, they decided to save for a house. They had been casually looking around on the Internet for possible places and were unable to find anything within their price range.

"I honestly think we were born too late," Raymond said. "The 1974 housing market—that was our time."

"Funny."

"We have the sort of jobs we could do anywhere. You wait tables, and I build decks."

"I'm not leaving LA."

"We should keep it in mind. If we want a house."

"I love LA."

"Nobody loves LA."

"I do."

"Maybe, but no one is silly enough to say it."

"I am."

"Except you."

***

While Sophia flossed her teeth in the bathroom in front of the mirror, Raymond paced around the bedroom mumbling.

"I can't hear a thing you are saying."

He walked into the bathroom, a little too quickly, as if there were an emergency, and said, "I think we should think about having a baby."

Sophia looked at her strand of floss, then put it between the next set of teeth, moved it back and forth, slid it out, and looked it over again.

"OK."

She flossed all her top teeth, rolled up the strand, tossed it in the trash, pulled out the next strand, wrapped it around the two metal prongs, and yanked. She looked at herself in the mirror.

"I guess I should get a checkup," she said. "I'll stop taking the pill. You should buy some condoms."

"When do we start doing it for real?"

Sophia laughed, leaned over, and kissed his cheek. "I'm glad I brought you down from the heavens to me."

He kissed her cheek and patted her on the butt on his way back to the bedroom.

***

In the middle of the afternoon, Raymond walked into the apartment and said, "I have something for you to come and see."

Sophia looked up from the couch, cross-legged, a large art book open on her lap. She was peeling strands from a stick of string cheese, layering them in her mouth.

"Now?"

"Yes."

"Right this minute?"

"Yes. Hurry up. Put some shoes on."

He took her on a drive through Beverly Hills, down Sunset Boulevard, a few quick turns, and he pulled over, parking on a street with early twentieth-century mansions. They walked up to a large, lovely dilapidated house with overgrown foliage. There were work signs tacked up to the left and right and a broken Porta-Potty in the driveway.

It was a Mediterranean-style home with the curved red spanish roof tiles, discolored and damaged cream stucco walls.

"Please tell me you didn't buy this. Please."

"I could tell you that, but it would be misleading."

"Without consulting me?"

"Just wait a minute. Let me take you through it. And it's not ours to keep. It's an investment, but we can live in it while I fix it up."

It was a remarkable home. She did want to see inside.

"OK. I'll have a look around. But then I'm killing you."

"A little good-hearted killing never hurt anyone."

"This will hurt."

They walked from room to run-down room. Missing floorboards. Wallpaper peeling off the walls. Water stains on the ceiling. But there were four expansive bedrooms. A large kitchen. Lots of storage space.

"It has good bones," he said.

"Don't talk."

She peered out the windows into the overgrown but healthy yard. Scattered dead leaves covered the grounds. "When was the last time someone cleaned up out there?"

He scratched at the back of his head. "It's been a while. But that's why we're getting such a good deal."

"Is that an avocado tree?"

"Yes. And there are two orange trees."

She pursed her lips. "It's a little spooky."

"I thought that would be a plus."

"What's it like at night?"

"I've never been here at night."

"Just because I like those old movies doesn't mean I want to live in one."

She bent down and lifted up a corner of rotten rug. The wood floors underneath were pristine. She lifted a bit more rug. "Is that an inlay?"

He laughed.

She dropped the rotten rug and wiped her dirty hand on her jeans.

She stood at the window. "What will you do with the little swimming pool there?"

"I'm researching it."

"How much money did we put in?"

"All of it."

"All of it? And that was enough?"

"That's funny. No. My boss and my mother also put money in."

"Great."

"Hold on. There's more. Let me show you your painting studio out back."

"All our money?"

"Every pretty penny."

The painting studio was an old pool house, large and full of light. Two impressive but broken french doors opened to the small, empty swimming pool. Behind the studio was a brick wall covered in thick rosebushes.

It was a spectacular mansion. A disaster. But a beautiful one. It was large and gorgeous. It was a dream.

"Good thing I love it."

"I knew you would love it."

"What if I hadn't?"

"We have three days to back out, so it would've been OK."

"How long do you have to fix it up?"

"Two years at most. All I got to do is get it in shape. Make it presentable. I'll do the kitchen first, the master bed and bath, we'll move in, and then bing, bang, bong."

"Are they paying you?"

"No. This is extracurricular."

"So, it's late into the night every night?" She walked over to a closet door and opened it. "I can help."

"Why not! It'll be fun. You do know how to nail things." He winked.

"I nailed you."

"I know. I was there."

"How'd we get so lucky?"

"I don't know."

***

It did not take Raymond long to fix up the master bedroom and bath. The plumbing wasn't as damaged as he first thought. The kitchen was a smooth process as well. Sophia ripped up all the rotten carpet and pulled out all the staples with pliers. They hired landscapers to bring in a crew to clean up the yard. Once Sophia had rolled up all the carpet and taken it to the Dumpster in the driveway, Raymond hired a crew to come in and clean the house.

"Can we have someone clean the windows?"

"Of course."

Within seven weeks, they were moving in their things. They brought in their bedroom furniture, their dining room table and chairs, their sofa. Sophia put all her artwork in her studio. She built shelves to store her canvases on their sides. She set up her paintbrushes. Her paints. A stack of canvases to the right waiting to be painted upon. A stack of cheap white work towels.

The last thing they removed from their apartment was their large wedding backdrop of the earth and the moon. They folded it carefully. Wrapped it in thick clear plastic. Taped it up. They carried it out, down the elevator, and put it in the bed of the truck.

***

Sophia was fondest of the mansion in the daytime, but once night fell, the feel of the house shifted. Most of the electricity didn't work, and she'd have to move from room to room with flashlights or camping lamps or candles, and it seemed as if she had survived a natural disaster of some sort. The house was empty and broken. The shadows were long, and the noises of the house were unfamiliar.

If the wind blew just right, a sound like that of a baby crying could be heard. It turned out to be a broken spanish roof tile that Raymond removed and replaced. She knew it was something innocuous like that, but the noise had to be stopped all the same.

It wasn't easy for Sophia to get to work from the new house. It was three bus rides, and she wasn't used to that. She liked walking to and from work. It also added two hours to her day.

*** 

One weekend morning Sophia felt sick.

Raymond said, "You're pregnant. You need a cracker."

He brought in an unopened sleeve of saltines and set it beside her on the bed.

"Can I have some hot tea?"

He returned with a cup of tea on a matching saucer. "Where are the pee sticks?"

Sophia sat up in bed. Half the crackers had been eaten. She brushed the crumbs to the floor. She had a sip of tea.

Raymond returned with a pregnancy test stick and a plastic mixing bowl from the kitchen. He held up the stick and said, "For your urine." He held up the mixing bowl, "For your vomit."

"The body is so fun," Sophia said.

"When we get a baby, that's going to be the funnest part of all."

"Don't get too excited."

"I know you're pregnant. I know it."

"I'm just going to sit here and drink my tea and eat my crackers. You should find something else to do."

"Are you nuts? And miss one of the best moments of my life?" He lay back on the bed and stretched out his arms. "We might be having a cute little baby."

"We might not."

"I got very powerful semen. It's like rocket-science semen."

"That's adorable."

He turned on his side facing her. "Are you ready?"

"I'm ready."

They got up from the bed and walked to the bathroom. Sophia pulled down her underwear, sat on the toilet seat, opened the pregnancy stick, looked up at her husband, and said, "You can't stand over me like that. With your arms all crossed like Mr. Clean."

"What do I do?"

"Sit *there*."

He sat at the edge of the bathtub.

She peed on the stick as he leaned in and watched. "This is exciting," he said.

"You're in for a surprise," she said. "Get it? Urine. You're in?"

"I get it. It's not that amusing."

A little pink plus sign showed up within seconds.

"I knew it."

"This is faulty. It's not supposed to be that fast."

"You're just super pregnant."

"Yes, there's pregnant, super pregnant and sort of pregnant. I'm going to do it again."

She peed on eight sticks and all eight had pink plus signs.

"I knew it."

***

Her morning sickness was continuous. All day. All night. The scent of most everything made her queasy. She kept a piece of ginger root in her pocket and would smell it all day long. Snap it in half or, when it was too small to break, just scratch at it to release that refreshing scent. She'd close her eyes and breathe deeply.

He worked on the house, and she waited tables and prepared their bedroom for the baby.

Spending all day on her feet made her ankles swell and her back hurt. Riding the bus to and from work was torment. The smell of other people. Their sweat. Their perfume. Their old, dirty sneakers with the sour-yet-sweet smell of feet. Their underarms and the deodorant to cover that up. The plates of food she was putting on people's tables. The scent of her studio. Fresh paint. All of it was disgusting.

Late at night, alone in the bedroom while Raymond fixed plumbing or electricity or knocked plaster off a wall, she read as many baby books as she could. Sometimes she had to read by candlelight. The window by her bed slightly open, the cool night air filtering in. Raymond would be on the east end of the house, but sounds would be coming from the west. Raymond would be clanking away in the kitchen, but something would be scratching on the outside of the wall above her headboard. Sometimes there was a verifiable reason for the unnerving activity. A rat scurrying across the floor. Or a piece of exposed, rotten lath falling from the wall.

She could scare herself into a frenzy. Raymond would find her fully clothed, sitting uncomfortably on the toilet with the lid down. "You know you're supposed to lift the lid and pull your pants down first?"

"It's colder in here," she'd say, or "I thought I might be sick." But she simply found it the safest room in the house.

***

They saw a set of four midwives who rotated their duties. They might all be there for the birth or just one. They were all older ladies, new age hippies. Experienced. Open-minded. No-nonsense.

During the ultrasound, Sophia and Raymond were asked if they wanted to know the sex of their baby. They said no. The technician said, "Let's say you have a boy. Do you know how you both feel about circumcision?"

They did not.

"It's a really good idea to decide these things before the birth."

When the images were printed out, Sophia examined them closely. "Are you sure that's a vagina?"

The technician said he was.

Sophia pinned the images to the kitchen wall. She liked looking at the baby's spine. This fantastic detailed curve down the back. Like a rattlesnake tail.

*** 

Sophia's body became large and unwieldy. She didn't know how to move it anymore or where its boundaries were or where her center of balance was. She felt as if her body had been taken over not only by the baby but by her own skin. She felt weak and tired.

Late one night, a noise startled her awake. She sat up as fast as she could, which wasn't fast at all. First, she had to get up on her elbow, then she had to pull her legs in, then she had to push herself up, then pull her legs in even closer. This body was awful.

The candle beside her was flickering a long flame. Stretched shadows undulated on the walls and ceiling. So much of the room was hidden. She heard another, different noise. Like a shuffling. "Is that you?" she called out. The noise again. "Is that you?" her voice becoming shrill. Something she couldn't see entered the doorway. Her heart squeezed shut.

Then a foot came into the light of the candle flame,

a work boot, and then Raymond's voice. He had a glass of ice water in his hand. "It's just me. Calm down."

"I thought it might be something else." She laughed.

"There are no more rats. I promise."

"I was thinking more like a ghost."

"There are no such things as ghosts."

"Yes, there are. I know there are." She took a sip of water and set it on the nightstand.

"How do you know?"

"You. You're one of them." She watched his face closely. He smiled sweetly, put his hands on his hips.

"Why are you so crazy?"

"I don't know." She got on her elbow and slowly lowered herself. She put her head down on the pillow and cried. "I'm just pregnant is all."

"I'm not a ghost, honey. I have a social security number and everything."

***

Sophia and Raymond sat at their dining room table in the remodeled dining room. They did the math to figure out when she could quit her job. The baby seemed to be constantly stepping on her bladder. "I think she's tweaking it like one of those bicycle horns. *Beep beep beep*, out of the way, lady."

The swelling in her ankles never fully subsided. "I can't. I can't keep working like this."

"We didn't plan it right," Raymond said.

"I know. I meant to be born rich. Sorry."

"Me too!"

"Honey, I have to quit. I'm telling them tomorrow."

"When's the soonest you could go back to work? Because the math is saying you should be waiting tables while giving birth."

"Order up."

***

They borrowed money from their parents and got two new credit cards. One card had a seven-thousand-dollar limit, the other twelve. A very pregnant Sophia smiled. "Problem solved!"

"I feel sick," said Raymond.

"Now we understand each other."

***

Sophia waddled over to the kitchen sink, filled the kettle with water, put it on the stove, turned the knob *click click click,* then flame. She took two delicate teacups from the cupboard and two saucers. She spooned loose tea leaves into the metal filter. When the water was boiling, she poured it into the glass teapot, closed the lid, and set her phone alarm for five minutes. As she stood there, she listened to Raymond hammering away above her. She was due nine days ago. She'd been having labor pains on and off for the last few days. They would get excited, call the hotline, only to have the nurse on the phone tell them that it wasn't time yet. Raymond would write down the rules again and hang up. The contractions would fade.

The midwives were talking about inducing.

When the alarm on her phone went off, Sophia poured the tea into the cups. Just after that, a little bit of warm liquid spread across her underwear. She looked down, but all she could see was her belly. She felt her crotch, looked at her hand. No blood. She smelled her hand. It just smelled like crotch. She called out, "I think maybe my water broke, or I peed myself."

Raymond called back from a room above, "What?"

Then a bunch of liquid plopped from her body to the kitchen floor. She called out, "My water broke!"

Raymond ran down the stairs and into the kitchen.

"Careful," she said.

He grabbed a dish towel, tossed it on the floor. Sophia stepped on the towel and swished it around, cleaning up the fluid.

"That means we go, right?"

"Get my bag."

***

Giving birth took hours. At one point, when Sophia was on her hands and knees on the examining table—red-faced and sweaty, tears drying on her cheeks, drool falling out of her mouth—one of the nurses had Sophia's hospital gown gathered up and held in the air while two other nurses, knees bent slightly, peered into Sophia's backside.

Raymond leaned into Sophia's ear and said, "It's like football. It's a huddle. They're calling a play."

Sophia turned her head. "You, Raymond, are making me...regret...ever bringing you...down from up there."

Raymond stepped back.

The nurses, heads tilted, watched him.

"She's always saying stuff like that." He shrugged.

One of the nurses put her hand on Sophia's ass and said, "Stop bearing down."

Sophia, clenching her teeth, asked, "How?"

At one point the four midwives gathered in a far corner, whispering.

Raymond leaned toward Sophia, "This is more Shakespearean. Like witches. At a cauldron."

The midwives walked over in unison, each grabbing

Sophia by a different body part, and flipped her onto her back as if she were a piece of furniture—like a coffee table. Raymond watched one of the women slide her fingers into Sophia's vagina, turning her hands to the right and then the left, her fingers gliding ever deeper in. The midwife got a hold of the baby and pulled it out.

Raymond said, "Wow."

The baby was silent.

Sophia was silent.

Raymond was supposed to cut the umbilical cord, but that didn't happen.

They took the baby to the counter, put it under the heat lamp. Raymond talked to the little silent baby from a distance. He looked over the little hands and the little feet. The nurse poked the bottom of the baby's foot, but the baby didn't cry. The baby didn't seem to be moving.

The nurse suctioned each nostril, then the mouth. Someone said something about a low score. The midwives peered over the nurse and watched.

The tallest midwife said, "We should take her."

Another midwife said, "Wait. Just wait."

Sophia called out from the hospital bed, "Where's my baby? How's my baby? Where's my baby?"

At the sound of Sophia's voice, the baby moved. The more Sophia talked, the more the baby perked up.

One of the midwives brought Sophia the newborn wrapped in a white blanket with turquoise and magenta stripes running across it. Raymond cuddled up next to his wife and child. The nurses left the room. Sophia kissed the baby's head and said, "You're a nice creature, aren't you?"

*** 

Sophia had no trouble breastfeeding. All the nurses were

very proud. Which made Sophia feel uncomfortable. The nurse who took care of her overnight had said, "The woman two doors down—her nipples are all wrong."

Sophia heard the morning nurse who had just left her room say to someone else in the hallway, "This one here—the baby latches right on."

Sophia wanted privacy. To just be alone with her baby. No one watching or judging or directing or comparing or shouting about them to others out in the hallway.

Sophia's mom came to visit from Berlin. She did not want to hold her granddaughter.

"What's her name?" She peered over and moved the blanket out of the way to get a look at the baby's sleeping face.

"Flora."

"What kind of name is that?"

Raymond's mom came to visit too. The first thing she did when she walked in was wash her hands and ask to hold the baby. Having both moms in the small room at the same time was overwhelming.

Raymond's mother sniffed the newborn's head. "I love the smell of babies."

Sophia's mother said, "Don't they basically smell of sour breast milk?"

"Did you keep the afterbirth?" asked Raymond's mom.

Raymond, hands in pockets, looking down at the floor, nodded.

"Oh my God," said Sophia's mother. "Are you going to eat it?"

"We're going to plant it in my garden," said

Raymond's mom. "By the cherry tree."

"That's still weird," said Sophia's mom.

A nurse walked in, looked over the baby in Raymond's mother's arms, then walked over to Sophia, felt her breasts, told Sophia to feed the baby from the right breast next time, took Sophia's vital signs, then squeezed her stomach with both hands like she was working with bread dough, punching it down.

When the nurse left, Raymond's mother said, "What on earth was that?"

"She's a strange one," said Sophia.

"But what'd she do to your belly?"

"She's wringing out my uterus. Getting it back to its proper size. Squeezing all the blood out."

Sophia's mother said, "That's absolutely disgusting."

"Turns out," Sophia said, "having a baby is kind of gross."

*** 

It was so nice to be with such a small, sweet baby. Delicate. Soft. Warm. This baby had the sweetest face. The cutest nose. The tiniest toes. The neatest fingernails. Pretty eyelashes. Her breath was delightful. Her tongue was tiny and fresh pink and adorable. The top of her head smelled good too.

But there was also this new mother body, which was different from the new pregnant body. Her breasts were even larger and full of milk that leaked everywhere. There were bleary sleepless nights followed by bleary sleepless days followed by bleary sleepless nights. And the constant fretting over the baby. *Is she eating enough? Is she breathing? Is she too hot? Too cold? Is there really supposed to be that much mustard-yellow poop coming out of her teeny, tiny, little body?*

Even with the baby, it was easy for Raymond to work on the house. She slept through all the noises. He could hammer all night long, and the baby wouldn't notice. But Sophia noticed.

By the time the baby was walking, they were ready to put the mansion on the market.

They moved most of their things to storage. A wistful longing took over Sophia as she packed up her art studio with the baby on her hip in the sling. Sophia never painted anything while living there. She wondered if she would ever have time to paint again.

They moved in with Raymond's mother, who lived alone in a two-bedroom bungalow in Pasadena. It was cramped but temporary.

Raymond's mother was a therapist who had an office in Old Town Pasadena. She could walk to work and back easily. She was kind and conscientious but also very particular. She meditated in her living room every morning. Did yoga in her living room every evening. Her girlfriend lived a few blocks away. She also had a grandchild just a few months older than Flora. Both grandmothers enjoyed taking their grandkids out for a walk around the neighborhood together in strollers or the slings. Sophia spent this time showering or napping.

Raymond's mother loved to steam vegetables and mash them and feed little Flora, pretending the spoon was an airplane. She took great joy in scraping the food off the baby's closed lips and feeding that back to her.

\*\*\*

The mansion went up for sale just as the baby turned one. They celebrated, just the four of them, which seemed odd to Sophia, and she kept asking, "Is this normal? Isn't it supposed to be a big party?"

Raymond's mother said that it was perfectly fine and not to worry. "Look how happy she is."

Raymond hired a company to stage the property. Fresh flowers. Fancy curtains. Vintage furniture. They even managed to make the empty swimming pool look attractive. He was proud and sad at the same time. He envied all the people who were able to afford such a lovely home.

It sold during the broker's open.

Sophia and Raymond made enough money to pay off all the debt they had accrued plus save some money, but did not make enough to have a down payment for a house of their own.

"So, we go back to renting? We did all this, and we go back to renting?"

"But we lived in a Beverly Hills mansion for two years. Come on! It was great."

"That's not fair. Your mom made money. Your boss made money."

"We made a little bit of money."

"Not enough."

Rent had gone up in those two years, and they needed a larger place now, since they had a child.

"I'm very tired," Sophia said. "I don't want to talk about this anymore."

"I know you're disappointed. But everything's fine."

\*\*\*

They tried to find a house to rent because they wanted a yard, but they ended up in a two-bedroom apartment in a medium-sized complex. There was a community gym. A decent-sized swimming pool. Sophia found a job waiting tables two blocks away, working Friday and Saturday nights while Raymond watched little Flora. He continued to build decks during the day while she took care of the baby. The most lucrative jobs for Raymond were out in Malibu or Bel Air, but the traffic was brutal, and he didn't get home until late at night.

They lived as cheaply as possible. They bought everything used except for their socks and underwear. They got rid of their storage unit, selling or giving away what they couldn't fit into their apartment. Raymond's father let them store a number of things in his garage in exchange for Raymond building a structure for the father's new hot tub.

"I don't like your dad."

Raymond took off his baseball cap and then put it back on. "Your dad's not all that special, either."

"You've never even met my father."

"That's one of the reasons he's not all that special."

\*\*\*

For fun, late at night, while their kid slept, they'd search the Internet for fixer-uppers. They found the perfect house once, a foreclosure, but that was a frustrating waste of their time. The house was for sale, but it seemed there was no actual way to buy it. They filled out a stack of paperwork, turned over the same bank information numerous times, wrote many letters, but six months in, there was just more paperwork. They vowed to never fall for that bullshit again, no matter how dreamy the house.

\*\*\*

After a night of waiting tables, Sophia's feet would ache, and she'd have to sleep with her feet up on pillows in order to get the swelling in her ankles to go down. In the morning, her feet would be tender as she padded over to the bathroom.

"I can't be on my feet like this anymore. I really can't."

"We'll figure something out," Raymond said.

Raymond rubbed Sophia's feet, massaging peppermint lotion into her skin.

"I'm sorry this didn't work out like I wanted," he said.

Little Flora was fast asleep on the large futon mat on the floor of their bedroom. She was on her stomach, her head was crooked in an awkward way, and one knee was bent.

Sophia's eyes closed as Raymond pressed deep into the arch of her foot. "I'm still glad I went up there and got you."

\*\*\*

They celebrated Flora's second birthday out at the pool. In bathing suits. Flora with floaty water wings on her skinny arms and wearing a little yellow bikini, her belly button protruding out like a toy. When Flora was in arm's reach, Sophia would press her belly button and Flora would stick her tongue out.

It was just the three of them. They made the same cupcakes they had made for their wedding. Flora had her first taste of cake and didn't like it. They cut open a cantaloupe for her instead, and she happily ate that sitting at the edge of the pool with her feet dangling in the pale-blue water, fruit juice dripping down her chin.

\*\*\*

Sophia held Flora's left hand, and Raymond held Flora's right as they walked down the street to the park. Flora had on a little Winnie the Pooh backpack and new black patent leather Mary Janes. Every few steps, the little girl would stop so she could admire her shiny new shoes.

There were a lot of people at the park already. Raymond and Sophia laid down the blanket, and Flora sat in Sophia's lap. The little girl looked at the kids playing and pressed her hands together with glee. Her eyes were big. She looked at those other children as if they were some sort of delicious treat.

***

When she was three, Flora stopped sleeping at night. She wanted to play until she passed out. But Sophia kept a pleasant bedtime schedule anyway. Warm bath. Dimmed lights. Reading of books. Sometimes Sophia would read fifteen books and Flora would still be wide awake.

On this particular night, they heard keys jangling, then dropping, then Raymond cursing, then the keys in the lock again. The front door opening and closing.

"I think that's Daddy," Flora said.

"I think you are right, but it's time to sleep. Close your eyes. Lie down." Sophia put her hand on Flora's chest and pressed the child down, flat on her back. "It's time to sleep." Sophia pretended to make snoring sounds as Flora crawled out of bed and walked out of her room. Sophia stared up at the ceiling. She could hear Raymond and Flora talking but couldn't understand what they were saying. She got out of bed and walked out to the living room to see her husband and child seated at the dining room table, eating takeout and smiling.

Raymond said, "Try this," and he spooned some noodles into Flora's open mouth. She was sitting on the chair on her knees, her elbows on the table.

"It's one in the morning," Sophia said.

Raymond looked at the watch on his wrist and smiled. He shrugged one shoulder.

"This is yummy, Mommy. You should have some."

"It's one in the morning. I'm going to bed."

"Goodnight, honey," said Raymond.

"Sleep tight, Mommy," said Flora.

***

In late winter, just after putting Flora down for an unlikely nap, Sophia sat at their dining room table, opened up her laptop, and checked her e-mail. There was a message from the director of that horror film she'd worked on years ago. He said he was wondering if she still lived in LA. If she were available to work on a full-length feature film that was to start shooting soon. Sophia picked up her cell. Her hands were shaking. She wanted to work. She wanted to paint. She called him. Yes, she wanted the job. Yes, she could be right over. Yes.

She, of course, didn't have a car. One of the people living in the apartment building, one of the moms, drove for money. Sophia dressed, packed her bag, picked up sleeping Flora, spotted the woman sitting by the pool, talking on the phone. The woman helped Sophia set up the app, taught her how to use it, helped her order the ride.

From that point on, every morning Sophia and Flora rode the bus to the warehouse where the film was to be made. Flora would unpack her own little workstation that mimicked her mother's larger station. The two of them would stop and eat their snacks together. Later, they would stop and eat their picnic dinners together. Sophia would ask Flora's opinion, and Flora would ask her mother's opinion. Sophia would squat down and look over Flora's paintings. The little kid had talent.

On his way home from work, Raymond would swing by in his truck and drive them home. Flora always fell asleep in the car seat between them. She'd do her best to resist, but the lull of the vehicle was too strong. Raymond would carry Flora up to their apartment. Her sleeping head lolling, her mouth open, her little-kid breath warming his cheek.

***

In time they had the down payment for a house. They searched the Internet looking for damaged places that other people wouldn't want to put the time and money into, places that Raymond could fix up himself. But still, even the worst places were much too expensive.

They found out about a property from one of Raymond's coworkers whose father was being moved into an assisted-living community. If they both used the friend's agent, she would agree to take a lower percentage, which would then make the house affordable. Sophia and Raymond said yes. It was a run-down house, but charming. A three-bedroom ranch-style just off a busy street. A dead end. So no through traffic. Their backyard was small and up against a steep hillside. It was a good house and in a decent school district. They were pleased. Flora would be starting kindergarten in the fall.

They fetched their stored things from Raymond's father's house. Sophia took great delight in unpacking her paintbrushes and art books. In unfolding what Raymond now referred to as their *Space Opera Marriage Mural*. Hanging in her small studio, the backdrop was more like a curtain. It was too big for the room and had folds in it. But that didn't matter to her. She carefully set up her workspace. Everything in its place. She gave herself time and comforting pep talks. *No pressure. It's been a long time. Don't worry.*

Her mother came in from Berlin to see their new home. She stopped by one Saturday morning with housewarming gifts. Sophia took her mom on a tour of their little house.

"What's that?" Her mother pointed to the futon on the master bedroom floor.

"That's where Flora sometimes sleeps."

"But that's terrible."

"It's not a big deal. Half the time she's in bed with us."

"Your child should never share your bed."

Sophia guided her mother out of their bedroom to Flora's. "This is her room."

"It's a nice enough room. I wonder why she doesn't like it."

"You're a very old lady who moved all the way to Berlin to share a bed with someone, and yet you wonder why a teeny, tiny child doesn't want to sleep alone. Curious."

They drank coffee as Flora opened her presents at the breakfast table.

Each gift was wrapped in a plain white dish cloth.

"I brought them all the way from Germany."

Flora said, "Germany is in Europe."

"Very good! You taught her that?"

"No, Mom, she looked it up herself on Google."

"I meant was it you or Raymond who taught her that."

Sophia's mother switched seats and sat next to Flora. "I really like your bedroom, Flora. It's so cute."

"It is," said Flora.

"I bet it's fun to sleep there, isn't it? All by yourself. All night long. Like a big girl."

Flora shrugged. Sophia groaned.

"What's this?" Flora pulled a skipping rope out of a brown rectangular box.

Sophia's mother looked up at Sophia and said, "You don't know what a jump rope is?" It sounded like an accusation.

"It's a skipping rope, honey," Sophia held out her hand. "Let me see."

Sophia walked out the back doors to the deck. She held the rope out before her with the cherry-red wooden handles, one in each hand, the curve of the rope hanging at her ankles. She stepped over the rope as she looked over her shoulder at Flora, watching from the window. Sophia swung the rope over her head. She let the rope stop and then stepped over it. She did that a few more times. Then she jumped. She did a one-legged kicking hop, trading her feet. Then she jumped once and tried to make the rope go around her body twice before she landed on the ground, but she tripped. "Well," she said, out of breath, "it's been a long time."

"Not bad," said her mother, who took the rope and jumped it for thirty seconds just as boxers jump rope. Quickly, with the rope never touching the ground. Sophia's mother crossed the rope in front of her body and jumped easily through the little loop. The grandmother was only a little out of breath when she stopped.

"Wow, Grandma." Flora held out her hand for the

jumping rope.

"We have to cut it down for your size first."

Sophia grabbed a pair of scissors from a kitchen drawer. They measured and cut and restrung and made a knot with a little extra length just in case Flora grew overnight anytime soon.

"It's very good exercise for your heart."

"Yes, that's what she cares about, Mom. Cardiovascular health."

"It's true."

Flora spent the morning swinging the rope, letting it stop, and hopping over it. She carried it all day. She fell asleep holding it that night.

"She can't sleep with it," said Raymond. "She could choke herself."

"We'll take it from her once she's deep asleep. Don't worry."

"What if she wants to sleep with it every night?"

"Then we'll have a conversation about that."

Since Flora wanted to sleep with it the next night too, they made a special bed for the rope and set that little bed on top of the dresser. They kissed the rope good night three times. *One. Two. Three.*

***

While Sophia made peanut butter and jelly sandwiches for lunch, Flora skipped across the back deck. Anytime the child got a rhythm going, the rope would knock against a raised wood plank, tripping Flora.

They ate their sandwiches and drank their milk while sitting at the kitchen table. Sophia cut an apple in half.

"That's a nice smell," said Flora.

"It's sweet."

They ate around the core and tossed their halves in the compost bin when done. They washed their sticky hands at the kitchen sink. The gardenia-scented soap made their skin smell good, and they each took a moment to sniff the other's freshly clean hands.

"Why don't you practice in the garage? The floor in there is very smooth."

Sophia propped open the door from the house to the garage, then pressed the garage door opener. Flora covered her ears to block the loud sound of the garage door being pulled up to the ceiling. There was now fresh air and light.

"That's better." Sophia kissed Flora on the cheek. "I'm going to paint, OK?"

"Yes, Mommy."

Sophia watched her daughter skip around the garage in her little dark-blue sundress with the little white daisies. Her bright-green sandals. "Stay in here, OK?"

Flora skipped from one side to the other by swinging the rope and stepping over it. Every once in a while, she'd stop and try to jump the rope and then move on to running and hopping over it. She sang songs. She talked to herself. She'd skip down the driveway and then back up. Skip down, skip up. She'd stop to pet the grass as if it had feelings and needed some attention. She'd stop to watch an ant. She'd just stare off into the bright-blue sky. Watch the fluffy clouds.

A car stopped at the bottom of the driveway. A man leaned out the open window and asked Flora what her name was. She was just about to throw the rope over her head. She rested her hands on her shoulders, the rope dangling down, bouncing off the back of her legs. She looked at him but said nothing. He opened the car door and stepped out. He was in no hurry. He stretched.

"Me and my friend here used to live on this street when we were little kids."

Flora said nothing. She stayed very still. He took a few steps over to the left. He was not any closer to her. "Oh, gosh," he said. "Riding in a car sure does get uncomfortable."

Flora turned her head. She looked to her house.

"Hey, kid, hey, do you like kittens? We have a box of kittens right here."

She didn't believe him. She frowned.

"Honest!"

He walked to the back of the car, reached into the back seat, and pulled out a cardboard box.

"Come and see."

Flora took a step away from him. He laughed. He put the box on the ground and tilted it so she could see inside. He walked closer to her. She stepped toward him. He shook the box. There were kittens in there. Five of them. Five fluffy cute kittens. She looked up at him, and he smiled.

"You can pet them," he said. He squatted down, set the box on the driveway, and she bent down and ran her little hand over their soft, small bodies.

"I'd let you hold one, but I don't want it to jump away and get lost."

Flora looked up into his face. She could imagine the pleasure of one of those little furry bodies in her actual hands.

"You could hold one in the car. If you really want to

hold one. They can't get away in there."

She really wanted to hold one.

***

Standing at her easel, Sophia was slopping paint on her canvas. Anything. Painting whatever she felt like. A flower. A fence. A shoe. No pressure. Just getting paint on the canvas with the brush. She painted the view out her back window. The hillside.

She noticed that there was too much silence. There was so much of it that it was like a thing taking on a form, butting its way into this too-small room, shouldering itself in, pressing on her. She turned, paintbrush in hand, and walked out of the little back room, into the garage, and down the driveway. There was no Flora. Sophia didn't bother to call her name. She knew she was gone.

Sophia didn't look to her right, down the dead-end street. Instead, she turned left at the end of her driveway and walked as if she were drugged. She tried to run, but it was more like loping. The sadness was too much. She was crying. She couldn't breathe. There was a paintbrush in her hand. She looked at it as if she were trying to understand what it was. She fainted ever so gently, collapsing as if she were a simple bedsheet, so softly falling down to the hot, hard street.

As she lifted out of her body, she saw herself, there, splayed on the pavement. She saw a neighbor running out his front door—the older, retired man who was always doing yard work, cutting grass, clipping bushes. He was crossing the street in his socks. He was on his knees beside her body. There was a neighbor's car stopping now. Sophia turned away from all this and went up higher.

She knew the car was green. That it had four doors.

But she didn't know which way they went—if at the end of the street they turned left or right or drove straight ahead. She went higher. The car was green, dark green. It had four doors. It was long and squarish. It was an older car. She went higher. The car was green. It had dents and dings. Four doors.

She scanned the streets. How long had it been? How far could you get in just a few minutes? She went to the left, then the right, to the left, zigzagging. Anytime she spotted a green car, she'd swoop down, look inside, then up again. At a stoplight two blocks ahead, she saw an old dark-green car in the far-right lane. She flew down. Flora was there in the backseat with her hand in a box full of kittens. Flora was talking to the kittens ever so gently. Petting them ever so sweetly. The car turned right at the next street, then left into the second driveway and stopped. The passenger got out of the car. He was tall. His jeans were dirty and ripped. His sneakers were new and clean. He opened the back door of the car and pulled out the box. Flora scooted out and stood on the driveway and looked around. She was sucking on the end of one of the cherry-red handles of her jump rope. She had a kitten in the other hand, held tight to her chest. She looked nervous. The man shook the box of kittens and said, "You should pick one out. I bet your mom will let you keep one. Come on. Let's go inside and call her on the phone." He walked across the yellow, crunchy grass. Flora looked around, then followed.

The car pulled into the garage. The driver got out. He was short. He walked to the edge of the garage and jumped up to grab the red plastic bobble hanging from above. He caught it and yanked the garage door down. It was like the door to a tomb shutting. *Thump.*

Sophia opened her eyes. She was on the street again. She was being cradled by her neighbor, the older man. He was saying, "Don't worry. The ambulance is on the way."

Another neighbor, the woman in the house on the other side, had her hands on her hips and was saying, "Where's her little kid at?"

Sophia said, "Call the police." Her mouth was dry. She tried to swallow.

"Don't worry, the ambulance is on the way."

"Someone stole my baby."

The man dropped her as he stood up. "Someone stole the little girl. Call the police."

Sophia could move her right arm and turn her head, but she couldn't move her left arm or her legs. Her chest hurt. She needed something to drink. The older man got down on his knees again, and Sophia told him that he had to listen to her. She gave him the address. She said it was a stucco house. Just few blocks away. That all the grass in the front yard was dead. She held on to the man's shirt. She said, "Please, bring me my baby, please." It was much too difficult to breathe, to stay awake, so she closed her eyes and dreamed.

*** 

Sophia woke up in the hospital. It was a clean, bright room. She was tucked into the bed very tightly. The head of the mattress was raised up, and the TV was on, but there was no sound. It was a small room, and she was alone. She could move her right arm, and next to her hand on the bed was a remote. She pressed the button that said *Nurse.* Just a few seconds later, Flora came running into the room, yelling "Mommy, Mommy, Mommy," and leaping on the bed. Raymond walked in after.

They hugged. They kissed. Sophia drank from the water that Flora offered her.

Sophia said that she could not move her left arm or her legs. She said it as matter-of-factly as she could.

"You had a stroke," Raymond said.

"I had such a strange dream," she said. "I used to have this recurring nightmare. But it was different this time."

Raymond smiled. "Was it about Flora getting kidnapped?"

"This time it was."

"That wasn't a dream, honey. That happened."

Raymond was looking at her without blinking. He was watching her much too closely. "How did you know where she was?"

Flora got on her knees, "Mommy, listen, listen, they had kittens, Mommy, kittens."

"That's nice, Flora."

"But they were not nice men, Mommy. The kittens were a trick."

"Did they hurt you?"

Flora made fists out of her hands. "Never."

Raymond picked Flora up off the bed. "Do you know those men? How did you know where they lived?"

Sophia shook her head. Flora squirmed out of her father's arms and back on the bed. Sophia brushed at Flora's plump cheek with the back of her fingers.

"I don't understand," said Raymond. "How did you know?"

Sophia looked out the window.

"Until we had Flora," Raymond said, "I never felt

70

complete. I didn't feel real until I met you, and I never felt complete until we had our baby. When we were all in that hospital bed together and she was brand new, that's the first time I ever relaxed. The three of us. Do you understand me?"

"I do."

"Look at me."

Sophia turned her head.

"Then she was taken, and you were unconscious. I felt sick. I don't even have the words for it, Sophia. You've made me as crazy as you. I actually thought: Why did you come to the heavens and bring me down here?"

"I'm sorry."

"To ruin me?"

"No."

"I think I'm losing my mind."

"You're not."

"Do you know those men?"

"No."

"Then how did you know where they lived?"

She didn't say. It wasn't something she could tell him. It was something he would have to be shown.

The police assumed there was some nefarious activity happening between her and the kidnappers, although they had no proof.

The doctors said that they had a positive outlook for someone Sophia's age who had suffered a stroke. That she should regain most if not all of her motion. It was just a wait-and-see situation. And lots of rehab.

Sophia caught Raymond's reflection in the mirror above the sink. He was staring at her. When he noticed she was watching him, he smiled—it was sudden and false.

Later, he was putting the food tray on the counter, and she saw his reflection in the metal paper towel dispenser. He had that same distrustful gaze. She tried to move her body, turn away from him, but all she could turn was her head. She looked out the window. It was just bright-blue empty sky.

Late that night, she lay with Flora tucked up next to her in the hospital bed, playing with the finger puppets the nurses had given her earlier that day, the room dark except for a tiny light above the counter. Raymond was fast asleep in the chair by the window, slightly snoring, the beige blanket having fallen on the floor near his feet.

Two nurses were talking out in the hallway. Walking back and forth. Laughing. Their shoes squeaking across the linoleum.

Sophia nestled her head into her daughter's neck and whispered, "I have a secret."

Flora stopped playing with her toys and whispered, "Tell me."

"I can do something very special."

"What?"

"I can leave my body and float around. I can go anywhere in the world I want at any time I want."

"Anywhere?"

"Yes."

"Can you play up in the clouds?"

"Yes."

"Can you play at the bottom of the ocean?"

"I haven't, but I don't see why not."

"Teach me."

"I would love to."

"Can we teach Daddy too?"

"Of course we can."

Flora sat up on her knees, her back very straight. "What do I do to do it?"

"The first thing we do is close our eyes."

Flora tilted her head. "Are you trying to trick me? I'm not sleepy."

"No, I'm not. I swear."

Flora squinted her eyes, got comfortable on the bed again, leaned into her mother. "Not now," she said.

"Another time, then."

"Here." Flora placed the Big Bad Wolf finger puppet on her mother's chest. "Make a scary wolf voice and say about the huff and puff."

Sophia held out her index finger.

Flora laughed. "Sorry. I forgot." Flora reached over and gave her mother's paralyzed arm a nice little pat.

"You're very good to me," Sophia said.

"You're my mommy!" Flora put the wolf on her mother's finger.

Sophia growled and said, "I'll huff, and I'll puff, and I'll blow your house down."

"Scarier, Mommy. Be really, really scary."

Sophia growled. It came out much louder than she had expected. She looked over at Raymond to make sure she hadn't woken him. He was so soft there in the corner, fast asleep, slightly snoring, uncovered by the blanket. So vulnerable. Sweet. She was unable to do something so simple as get out of the bed, pick the blanket off the floor, and cover him. She needed to protect him. It was she who had found him in the heavens, and she had brought him down here to keep her company. She had been selfish. She needed to take care of him. She felt anger and fear and a strong force of violence. She wouldn't pretend to be the wolf. No. She said the line as she would say the line for real. She said it as if she were about to destroy someone's home. Someone's life. This was how she would speak to someone who had threatened her happiness. To someone who had threatened the people she loved. She said it in her own voice.

Flora plucked the puppet off her mother's finger.

"Too scary, Mommy. Too scary."